SHORT TALES
Furlock & Muttson Mysteries

THE CASE OF
THE SHIFTING STACKS

by Robin Koontz

magic wagon

visit us at www.abdopublishing.com

Published by Magic Wagon, a division of the ABDO Group, 8000 West 78th Street, Edina, Minnesota, 55439. Copyright © 2010 by Abdo Consulting Group, Inc. International copyrights reserved in all countries. All rights reserved. No part of this book may be reproduced in any form without written permission from the publisher.

Short Tales ™ is a trademark and logo of Magic Wagon.

Printed in the United States of America, North Mankato, Minnesota.
092009
012010

♻ PRINTED ON RECYCLED PAPER

Written and illustrated by Robin Koontz
Edited by Stephanie Hedlund and Rochelle Baltzer
Interior Layout by Kristen Fitzner Denton
Book Design and Packaging by Shannon Eric Denton

Library of Congress Cataloging-in-Publication Data

Koontz, Robin Michal.
The case of the shifting stacks / written and illustrated by Robin Koontz.
   p. cm. -- (Short tales. Furlock & Muttson mysteries)
ISBN 978-1-60270-563-0
[1. Libraries--Fiction. 2. Mystery and detective stories.] I. Title.
PZ7.K83574Cass 2010
[E]--dc22
                                                2008032531

"Good morning, Muttson!" Furlock said.
"Would you like some animal crackers?"
"Thank you," said Muttson.
"Take some with you," Furlock said.
"We need to go to the library."

"Do we have a case?" asked Muttson.
"No," said Furlock. "My library books are due!"
"I will fire up the Furlock-Mobile," said Muttson.
They sped to the library and went inside.

"I am returning my books," said Furlock.
"Yes, of course," said Mrs. Beazley, looking upset.

"What is the matter?" Furlock asked.

"We have a mystery!" said Mrs. Beazley.

"Furlock and Muttson Detective Agency, at your service," said Furlock.

Muttson got out his notebook and pen.

"What is your mystery?" asked Furlock.

"Books are moving around the library,"
said Mrs. Beazley.
"By themselves?" Furlock asked.
"It seems so," said Mrs. Beazley.

Furlock and Muttson followed
Mrs. Beazley to the stacks.
"Look at these books piled on the
floor," said Mrs. Beazley.

"These books are about rivers, ponds, worms, and wetlands," said Muttson, taking notes. "People leave books on the floor all the time," said Furlock. "That is no mystery."

"Well, come and look at these," said Mrs. Beazley. Furlock and Muttson followed Mrs. Beazley to the story time room.
"Look at these books piled against the wall," said Mrs. Beazley.

"These books are about fruit, grass, mud, and deserts," said Muttson, taking notes.
"Someone forgot their books after story time," said Furlock. "That is no mystery."

"Well, come and look at these," said Mrs. Beazley. Furlock and Muttson followed Mrs. Beazley to the reference room.

"Look at these hanging books," said Mrs. Beazley.
"Oh my," said Furlock. "This is very strange!"
"These books are about tall trees, berries, leaves,
and woodlands," Muttson said, taking notes.

"Muttson, please stop writing and pick me up," said Furlock.
Muttson lifted Furlock.
Furlock looked closely at the hanging books.

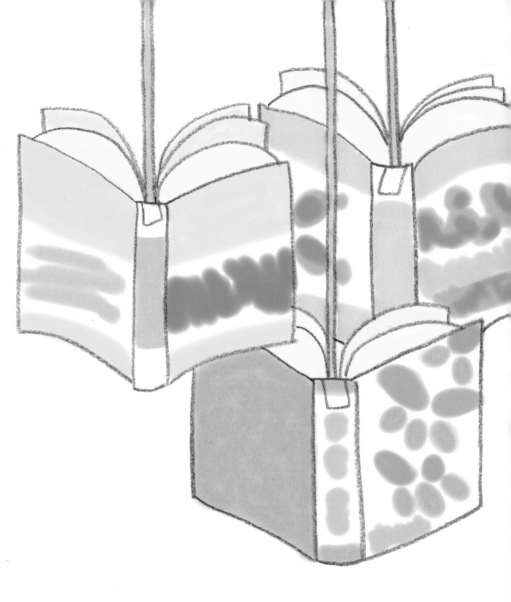

"What do you think is going on?" Mrs. Beazley asked.

"Please let me down, Muttson," said Furlock.

"I think I know what is going on."

"I think some kids are playing tricks," said
Furlock.
"Oh dear!" said Mrs. Beazley. "I saw two kids
giggling in the stacks earlier."
"We need to talk to them," said Furlock.

Mrs. Beazley left and came back with two kids. "What did we do?" cried the girl.

"Can you explain these hanging books?"
Furlock asked.
"We did not hang any books!" cried the boy.
Muttson flipped through his notepad.

"I think the kids are innocent," he said.
"How so?" Furlock asked.
"Who reads about rivers, ponds, worms, and
wetlands?" Muttson asked.

"Turtles," said Mrs. Beazley.
"Where are those books supposed to be?"
asked Muttson.

"In the stacks," said Mrs. Beazley. "But the turtles can't reach that high. I have to get the books for them."

"Who reads about fruit, grass, mud, and the desert?" Muttson asked.

"Elephants," said Mrs. Beazley.

"Where are those books supposed to be?" asked Muttson.

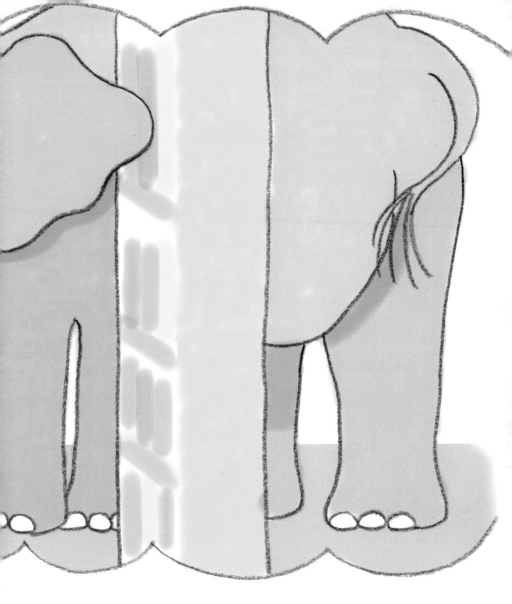

"In the stacks," said Mrs. Beazley. "But the
elephants can't fit between the rows. I have to
get the books for them."

"Who reads about tall trees, berries, leaves, and woodlands?" Muttson asked.

"Giraffes," said Mrs. Beazley.

"Where are those books supposed to be?" asked Muttson.

"In the stacks," said Mrs. Beazley. "But the giraffes can't reach that low. I have to get the books for them."
"Aha!" said Muttson.
"Aha what?" asked Furlock.

"Do you have a new helper who puts books in the stacks?" asked Muttson.
"Yes," said Mrs. Beazley. "His name is Chester."

Furlock and Muttson followed Mrs. Beazley
to the storage room.
"Chester, have you been shifting the
stacks?" asked Furlock.

"I just wanted everyone to be able to reach the books," Chester said.
"You did the right thing, Chester," said Mrs. Beazley.

"Our books should be easy for everyone to reach."
She patted Chester on the back.
"Mystery solved!" said Muttson.
"Thank you so much," said Mrs. Beazley.

"Muttson, do you still have those animal crackers?" Furlock asked.
"Yes, I do," said Muttson. "Have some!"
"On thoo thuh neth caseth!" said Furlock.
"I am right behind you," said Muttson.

They jumped into the Furlock-Mobile and sped away.